This Book Belongs to:

Mount Laurel Library
100 Walt Whitman Avenue
Mount Laurel, NJ 08054-9539
856-234-7319
www.mtlaurel.lib.nj.us

Mfg. by Leo Paper
Heshan, China
May 2013/PO#144476

Published in Nashville, Tennessee, by Tommy Nelson®, a Division of Thomas Nelson, Inc.

Tommy Nelson® books may be purchased in bulk for educational, business, fund-raising, or sales promotional use. For information, please e-mail SpecialMarkets@ThomasNelson.com.

Scripture quotations are from the *International Children's Bible*®, *New Century Version*®, copyright © 1986, 1988, 1999 by Tommy Nelson®, a Division of Thomas Nelson, Inc., Nashville, Tennessee 37214.

Library of Congress Cataloging-in-Publication Data

Higgs, Liz Curtis.
    Parable of the sunflower / by Liz Curtis Higgs ; illustrated by Nancy Munger.
        p. cm.
    Summary: Logan discovers how much good can come from the sunflowers he lovingly tends all summer. Text is interspersed with Bible verses.
    ISBN 10: 1-4003-0845-3 (2007 edition)
    ISBN 13: 978-1-4003-0845-3 (2007 edition)
    ISBN: 0-7852-7171-6 (1997 edition)
    [1. Sunflowers—Fiction. 2. Christian life—Fiction. 3. Parables.] I. Munger, Nancy, ill. II. Title.
    PZ7.H543955Pat 1997
    [E]—dc21
                                                                                            97—9998
                                                                                            CIP
                                                                                            AC

Printed in China

13 14 15 16 LEO 12 11 10 9

The Sunflower Parable

by
Liz Curtis Higgs

Illustrated by Nancy Munger

A Division of Thomas Nelson Publishers
Since 1798

www.thomasnelson.com

For our tall, sunny son,
Matthew Logan Higgs

Logan whistled his way down the lane toward home. He was counting the days until the summer sun would shine on his very own corner of the garden.

The farmer promised him that he could plant anything he wanted. And Logan wanted something B-I-G, bigger than his brother's cornstalks or his sister's hollyhocks. . . .

He wanted to grow great big sunflowers, so tall they would reach all the way to heaven!

"Look up at the sky and see.
Look at the clouds so high above you."
Job 35:5

After the warm sun of May chased the last frost away, Logan and the farmer chose the very best sunflower seeds.

"God is the One who gives seed to the farmer. . . .
And God will give you all the seed you need and make it grow."
2 Corinthians 9:10

"GIANT" declared the seed packet. Logan was sure his sunflowers would touch the skies by August.

"A person may think up plans. But the Lord decides what he will do."
Proverbs 16:9

Logan and the farmer worked side by side. They hoed the hard soil. They cleared the heavy rocks. They yanked out the pesky weeds that might choke the plants.

"A farmer does not plow his field all the time. . . .
He prepares the ground.
Then he plants the . . . seed."
Isaiah 28:24–25

The farmer added fertilizer. Logan pressed the tiny seeds down into the rich soil. Then the waiting began.

"A farmer is patient. He waits for his valuable crop to grow from the earth."
James 5:7

The warm summer rain brought fresh water. The sunflower seedlings poked their thirsty heads out of the soil.

"Drink! Drink!" Logan called from his window.

"The skies will send rain on your land at the right time."
Deuteronomy 28:12

The hot summer sun brought warmth and light,
which made the plants stretch taller.

"Grow! Grow!" Logan sang out.

How long until the flowers would bloom? How
long until they reached heaven?

"There is a right time for everything.
Everything on earth has its special season."
Ecclesiastes 3:1

Soon everything in the garden was growing very tall indeed.

His brother's cornstalks soared up, up, up.

"The deep springs of water made [them] tall."
Ezekiel 31:4

His sister's hollyhocks waved high above the fence.

But nothing grew taller than Logan's sunflowers. . . .

"Your love is so great it reaches to the skies.
Your truth reaches to the clouds."
Psalm 57:10

Whenever a breeze blew through the garden, the sunflowers nodded their heads.

"Yes!" they seemed to say. "We have B-I-G plans this summer."

"'I know what I have planned for you,' says the Lord."
Jeremiah 29:11

July turned into August without making a sound. The giant flowers turned their blossoms toward heaven. They followed the sun with their own round, brown faces.

"All living things look to you for food.
And you give it to them at the right time."
Psalm 145:15

"Soon my sunflowers will stretch all the way to heaven," Logan boasted. He was very proud of his hard work.

"You know that your work in the Lord is never wasted."
1 Corinthians 15:58

But at summer's end, the flowers suddenly stopped growing. Their faces, heavy with seeds, bent toward the ground.

Hungry birds hopped around the stalks.

"Like the grass, they will soon dry up.
Like green plants, they will soon die away."
Psalm 37:2

Logan grew very sad. The tallest flowers on his father's farm would never make it to heaven now. The tall corn would be cut down for harvest. The hollyhocks would soon bloom no more. All their work was good for nothing.

"What do people really gain from all the hard work they do here on earth?"
Ecclesiastes 1:3

The farmer knew his son was disappointed, but the farmer also knew a secret or two:

The corn would provide food for many people. The hollyhocks would bloom again next summer. And the sunflowers . . . ?

Well, the sunflowers were created with a gift inside: SEEDS! Seeds to feed birds. Seeds to feed people. Seeds to be carried all over the world, just as God planned.

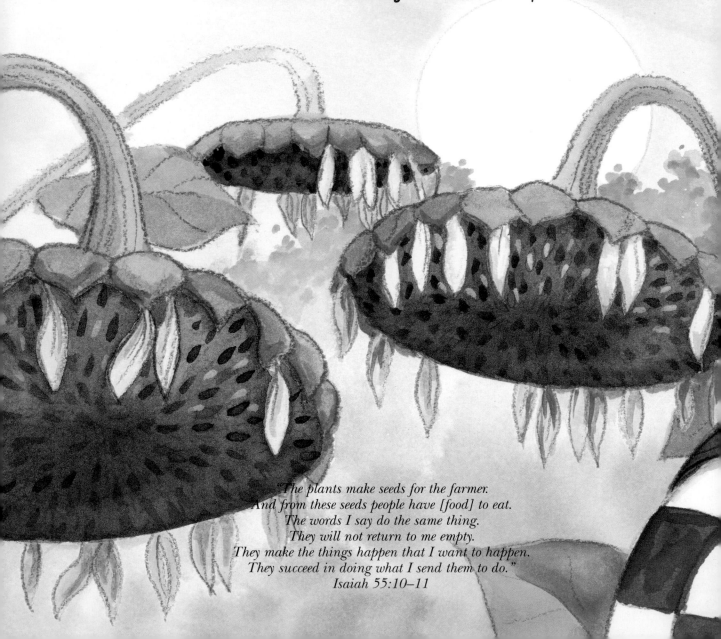

"The plants make seeds for the farmer.
And from these seeds people have [food] to eat.
The words I say do the same thing.
They will not return to me empty.
They make the things happen that I want to happen.
They succeed in doing what I send them to do."
Isaiah 55:10–11

"Look, my son," the farmer said. "See what a good harvest your sunflowers have produced."

"We must not become tired of doing good.
We will receive our harvest. . . .
We must not give up!"
Galatians 6:9

Logan watched as birds of every kind lifted the seeds right out of the sunflowers. The birds flew up, up, over the fields, off toward the horizon until they disappeared from sight.

"Look at the birds in the air. They don't plant or harvest. . . .
But your heavenly Father feeds the birds."
Matthew 6:26

"Father, the sunflowers reached heaven after all," Logan shouted with joy. "Those seeds will go everywhere."

"Everywhere in the world the Good News
is bringing blessings and is growing."
Colossians 1:6

The farmer nodded. "What can you do with the sunflower seeds that are left?"

*"Finish the work that you started.
Then your 'doing' will be equal to your 'wanting to do.'"*
2 Corinthians 8:11

Logan thought harder. "We can sprinkle our seeds with salt and share them with hungry friends!"

"Because we loved you, we were happy to share God's Good News with you."
1 Thessalonians 2:8

"And we can save some seeds to plant next summer," Logan said, pleased with himself for thinking such good thoughts. "Next year, let's plant twice as many seeds!"

Remember this: The person who plants a little will have a small harvest.
But the person who plants a lot will have a big harvest."
2 Corinthians 9:6

The farmer nodded once more and smiled. "See how much good we can do when we work together in my garden?"

"We are workers together for God.
And you are like a farm that belongs to God."
1 Corinthians 3:9